This book belongs to:

....

*for
everyone
who
smiles
in the
rain!*

**A big thank-you to my editor Peter Marley and
art director Jo Cameron for their inspiration and enthusiasm.**

Henry Holt and Company, *Publishers since 1866*
Henry Holt® is a registered trademark of Macmillan Publishing Group, LLC
175 Fifth Avenue, New York, NY 10010 • mackids.com

Library of Congress Control Number: 2016059605

Our books may be purchased in bulk for promotional, educational, or business use.
Please contact your local bookseller or the Macmillan Corporate and
Premium Sales Department at (800) 221-7945 ext. 5442 or by e-mail at
MacmillanSpecialMarkets@macmillan.com.

First published in 2017 by Oxford University Press
First American edition, 2017
The drawings in this book were created using watercolors, pencil, and calligraphy ink,
then collaged and colored using QuarkXPress and Adobe Photoshop.
Printed in China by Leo Paper Group, Gulao Town, Heshan, Guangdong Province

7 9 10 8 6

Singing
IN THE RAIN

BASED ON THE SONG BY
ARTHUR FREED AND NACIO HERB BROWN

PICTURES BY
timhopgood

GODWINBOOKS
Henry Holt and Company
NEW YORK

I'm **singing** in the rain,
just singing in the rain.

What a **glorious** feeling . . .

I'm **happy** again.

I'm laughing at clouds, so dark up above.

The sun's in my heart and I'm ready for love.

Let the stormy clouds **chase**

everyone from the **place.**

Come on with the rain . . .

I've a **smile** on my face.

I walk down the lane, with a **happy** refrain.

And I'm singing,

just singing

in the rain.

I'm **singing** in the rain,

just singing in the rain.

What a **glorious** feeling . . .

I'm
happy
again.

I'm laughing at clouds,
so dark up above.

The sun's in my heart
and I'm ready for love.

Let the stormy clouds **chase**

everyone from the **place**.

Come
on
with
the
rain . . .

I've
a
smile
on
my
face.

I walk
   down
      the lane,
         with a
            happy
               refrain.

And I'm
singing . . .

...just singing in the rain!

SiNGiNG
iN THE RaiN

**BASED ON THE SONG BY
ARTHUR FREED AND NACIO HERB BROWN**

I'm singing in the rain,
just singing in the rain.
What a glorious feeling,
I'm happy again.

I'm laughing at clouds,
so dark up above.
The sun's in my heart
and I'm ready for love.

Let the stormy clouds chase
everyone from the place.
Come on with the rain,
I've a smile on my face.

I walk down the lane,
with a happy refrain.
And I'm singing,
just singing in the rain.

Apart from "**SiNGiNG iN THE RAiN**" being the centerpiece to one of my favorite films, the reason I chose to illustrate this song is its underlying positive message. As adults, it is easy to forget the joy of rain.

We tend to view it as an inconvenience rather than the wonderful thing that it is. Rain is something beautiful that connects all life, from the city to the rain forest. So next time it rains, don't stay indoors. Go outside and soak it up like the children in this book. What a glorious feeling it is!